11/10 25 7/10

To my little sister Jess
—SL

For the Irvine Chimps
—JT

tiger tales
an imprint of ME Media, LLC
202 Old Ridgefield Road, Wilton, CT 06897
Published in the United States 2004
Originally published in Great Britain 2003
By Little Tiger Press
An imprint of Magi Publications
Text ©2003 Sam Lloyd
Illustrations ©2003 Jack Tickle
CIP data is available
ISBN 1-58925-035-4
Printed in Belgium

Yummy Yummy! Food for My Tummy!

by
Sam Lloyd

Illustrated by
Jack Tickle

tiger tales

Far, far away in the middle of the deep blue sea were two small islands.

On Banana Island there lived a little chimp named

George,

and on Coconut Island there lived a little chimp named

Jess.

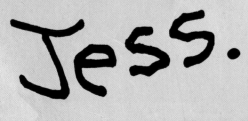

One day, George saw Jess and thought, "Wow, she looks friendly!"

And Jess saw George and thought, "Hey, he looks nice!"

And they both thought about how much fun it would be to share a banana milkshake and a piece of coconut cake.

But there was a problem.
In the deep blue sea between
the two islands there were . . .

... sharks!

" Yummy, yummy! Food for my tummy! "

the sharks sang when they saw the little chimps.

"Don't worry!" shouted George to Jess. "I have a plan. I'll make some wings from the leaves of my banana tree and fly across to visit you." George flapped and flapped his new wings. He jumped up and down but he couldn't fly.

" Yummy, yummy! Food for my tummy!" the sharks sang, snapping at George's little chimp toes.

"I've got an idea!" shouted Jess to George, excitedly. "I'll tunnel deep under the sea and come to visit you."

Jess dug and dug,
but the sharks heard
the digging noise.

**"Yummy, yummy!
Food for my tummy!"**

the sharks sang as they
smashed and bashed the
tunnel until it flooded.

"Never mind," called George. "I've got another idea!"

Jess watched as George tied slippery banana peels to his hands and feet and started to ski-surf across the water.

Jess knew that this was the silliest idea
so far, but before she could warn George . . .

he fell in!

"Yummy, yummy!
Food for my tummy!"

George swam faster and faster.
The sharks got closer and closer . . .

George made it back to Banana Island just in time!

"That was a close one," called Jess.

Jess soon thought of a brilliant plan. "This will scare the sharks away," she shouted to George. With a mighty roar she jumped out from behind the tree, waving her arms around. But the sharks were not in the least bit afraid. They found the crabby coconut costume very funny and laughed until their bellies ached.

"Yummy, yummy! Food for my tummy!"

"This is no good," thought the little chimps. "We've tried every idea in our heads. We need to think of something new if we're ever going to share milkshakes and cake!"

They both climbed up their trees—a very good place to go when you need to think.

As the chimps climbed higher and
higher, the trees began to bend.

The higher they climbed, the more the
trees bent . . . and bent . . . until . . .
"Oh no! We'll be eaten for sure!"

Then, something
amazing happened.
Their treetops met and
tangled tightly together
to form a big leafy knot.
"Hooray, we're
saved!" cried George
and Jess, high above the
horrible, hungry sharks.
And they were
together!
"Hi, George!" said
Jess.

"Hello, Jess!" said
George.

To celebrate their new friendship,
George and Jess had a party with music
and dancing. And of course lots of
banana milkshakes and coconut cake!